WWE Tag Teams and Team-Ups

Written by Steve Pantaleo

Editor Rosie Peet
Senior Designer Nathan Martin
Designer Lisa Sodeau
Pre-production Producer Siu Chan
Producer Louise Daly
Proofreader Kayla Dugger
Managing Editor Paula Regan
Managing Art Editor Jo Connor
Publisher Julie Ferris
Art Director Lisa Lanzarini
Publishing Director Simon Beecroft

First American Edition, 2019
Published in the United States by DK Publishing
345 Hudson Street, New York, New York 10014

Page design copyright © 2019 Dorling Kindersley Limited
DK, a Division of Penguin Random House LLC
19 20 21 22 23 10 9 8 7 6 5 4 3 2 1
001–312634–March/2019

A catalog record for this book is available from the Library of Congress.

ISBN: 978-1-46547-972-3 (Paperback)
ISBN: 978-1-46547-973-0 (Hardback)

DK books are available at special discounts when purchased in bulk for sales promotions, premiums,
fund-raising, or educational use. For details, contact: DK Publishing Special Markets,
345 Hudson Street, New York, New York 10014
SpecialSales@dk.com

Printed and bound in China

A WORLD OF IDEAS:
SEE ALL THERE IS TO KNOW

www.wwe.com
www.dk.com

Contents

The New Day

Meet the WWE Superstars

WWE Superstars are tough athletes. They compete in the ring to be the best.

Bayley and Sasha Banks

The Bar

Sometimes Superstars team up to form a tag team. They can team up with friends or even a member of their family.

What is a tag team?

Tag teams are groups of two or more Superstars. They take part in matches together.

One Superstar from each team battles at a time. When they want to swap places, teammates touch hands. This is called making a tag.

The Bar

Working together

Superstars often wear matching outfits to show they are a team.

The Usos

Switching places during a match stops Superstars from getting too tired. Here, Finn Balor tags his teammate, Braun Strowman.

Making the tag

There are different ways to make a tag. Here are three.

Legal tag

A Superstar touches their teammate's hand to make a tag. This is a legal tag.

Blind tag

Sometimes a Superstar tags in without his opponent seeing. This is a blind tag.

Illegal tag

Superstars must tag from the corner of the ring. A tag from the middle of the ring is an illegal tag!

Mega moves

Teammates combine their strength to perform amazing moves.

Gallows and Anderson hold an opponent above their heads. Then they slam him into the mat!

Twin power

The Bellas are identical twins. They have a trick to surprise their rivals. When one of them is tired, they secretly switch places. Their rivals don't realize they are fighting a fresh Superstar!

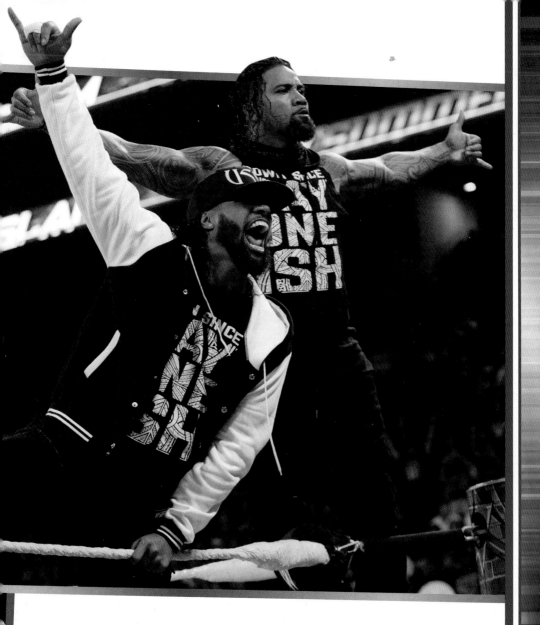

The Usos are also twins. They can each guess what the other will do next.

The New Day

Tag threes

The New Day has three members.
The Shield has three members, too.
They compete in three-on-three
matches.

The Shield bump fists before their matches. They are ready to compete as a team!

The Shield

Unusual team-ups

Sometimes Superstars team up with their opposites, or even their enemies!

Former enemies

Sheamus and Cesaro used to be enemies. Now they are tag team champions!

Different styles

The Rock likes to be cool. Mankind is a rebel.
Together, they make a winning team!

Hotheads

Daniel Bryan and
Kane often
argue with each
other. They have
won many matches.

Tag team titles

Tag teams fight for the *RAW* and *SmackDown* Tag Team Championships. The best team wins the title.

Dolph Ziggler

Titles are special belts. Winning teams wear their titles with pride! Dolph Ziggler and Drew McIntyre show off their titles.

Drew McIntyre

Match rules

WWE referees are always watching out for trouble. Breaking rules can get a tag team disqualified!

Only one Superstar from each team can wrestle at a time.

Once a tag is made, teammates have five seconds to switch places.

If a Superstar is pinned down, their partner can enter the ring. They have five seconds to help them.

The referee tells Jey Uso he has broken the rules!

23

Bending the rules

Sneaky teammates sometimes help from outside the ring. Here, Billie Kay pulls her teammate Peyton Royce away from Asuka's grasp.

Here, Drew McIntyre stops Finn Balor from climbing. If the referee sees him, he will be disqualified!

Hall of fame

Here are some of WWE's most famous teams. Some are from WWE history. Some are still fighting today!

New Age Outlaws

These rebels always caused chaos in the ring.

D-Generation X

Triple H and Shawn Michaels were not afraid to bend the rules!

The Hart Foundation

Bret "Hit Man" Hart and Jim "The Anvil" Neidhart were a super-strong team.

The Hardy Boyz

These brothers are hard to beat!

The Dudley Boyz

This tough team like to slam their enemies through tables!

Stables and factions

Sometimes a few Superstars join together. These groups are called stables and factions.

Finn Balor formed the Balor Club with his friends.

The Four Horsewomen inspire other female Superstars. They are strong and fearless!

SAnitY

SAnitY are a scary faction! They look spooky and they fight hard.

The members of SAnitY wear dark clothes. They paint their faces to scare their opponents.

The Riott Squad

Ruby Riott formed the Riott Squad with Sarah Logan and Liv Morgan. Their goal was to beat Charlotte Flair. Now, they want to beat everybody!

This fierce faction will do anything to win. They even attack their rivals backstage!

33

Survivor Series

At *Survivor Series*, teams from *RAW* and *SmackDown* battle. They battle until only one Superstar remains.

Team from *RAW*

Teams from *RAW* wear red.
Teams from *SmackDown* wear blue.
The winner gets to boast about
being number one!

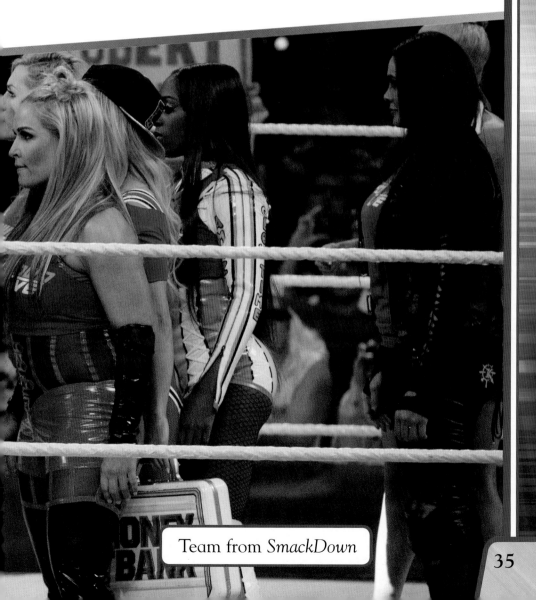

Team from *SmackDown*

The Usos

Face-off

Rival teams often trade insults before a match. Here, The New Day face off against their main rivals, The Usos.

The New Day

Multi-team matches

A match between three teams is
called a Triple Threat Match.
A match with four teams is called
a Fatal 4-Way.

Here, the Bludgeon Brothers take on The New Day and The Usos in a Triple Threat Match. Rowan leaps on Kofi Kingston and Jey Uso!

Tag team trouble

Even the best tag teams can fall out. Sometimes, teammates become jealous of each other.

Charlotte Flair and Becky Lynch used to be a team. They stopped getting along. Now, they are foes.

41

Champions

The Usos have won the *SmackDown* Tag Team Championship title three times.

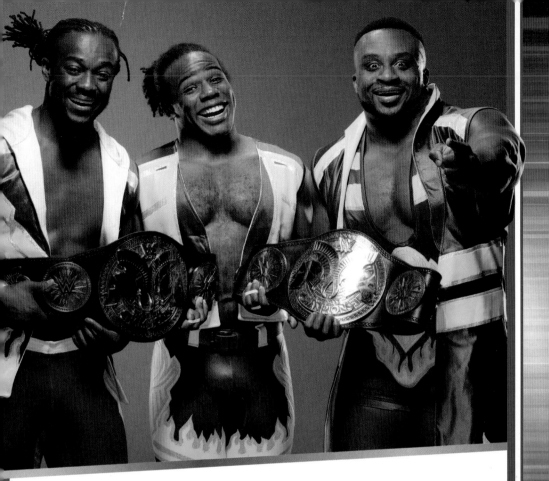

The New Day were the longest reigning champions. They held the title for 483 days! Champions need to watch out. There will always be another team ready to take their title!

Quiz

1. What kind of tag is made without a Superstar's opponent seeing it?

2. True or false: The Bellas are identical twins.

3. How do the members of The Shield show they are ready to fight together?

4. Which risk-taking Superstar did The Rock team up with?

5. What are the special belts that Superstars win called?

6. How long do Superstars have to switch places after they have tagged each other?

7. What is the name of the stable formed by Finn Balor?

8. Which faction wear face paint to scare their opponents?

9. Which Superstar formed the Riott Squad with Sarah Logan and Liv Morgan?

10. At *Survivor Series*, what color do teams from *RAW* wear?

Answers on page 46

Glossary

disqualified
Named the loser of a match after breaking a rule.

foes
Enemies.

identical twins
Twins that look exactly alike.

illegal
Against the rules.

opponent
Someone a Superstar fights against in a match.

Answers to the quiz on pages 44 and 45:
1. A blind tag 2. True 3. Bump fists 4. Mankind
5. Titles 6. Five seconds 7. The Balor Club 8. SAnitY
9. Ruby Riott 10. Red